things you need :

a pen

a penholder

a good pair of eyes

draw
a triangle

add
a vertical
line

and
another

and also
a few little
horizontal lines
(3 or 4)   roughly

on both
sides

there you go!

what about
the body?

oh yes!
I forgot
the body!
silly me ..

yes

so
to add the
body, you need
to separate
the beak from the legs

no way!

oi!

Ok, well.
the beak
and the legs
have gone.

we can
still draw
the body.
we start from
one end . .

and then
we turn around
first, the head...

.. followed
by the back ..

.. then the
tail ..

...and the tummy.
oh look, the beak and
the legs are coming back

and we finish
with the neck.

what about
the wings?

the wings?

oh yes, we need
to add wings!
there you go. a bit like
the tail but on the side.

what about
the eyes?

oh yes the eyes !
eyes are easy, two
dots and that's it.

and there it is!
a chicken. bravo!

now that you've drawn
a chicken, you can easily
draw an egg.

draw an oval

and there is your egg.
easy isn't it?

you can even
add legs
if you want...

and even eyes!
why not?

and what about a cockerel?
you can draw a cockerel too.
it's easy for you now.

draw a crest. it's a bit
like a floppy crown or
a glove with six fingers.

and a triangle for the beak
like we had at the beginning.

don't forget the body!
it's important for the cockerel.
so, same as before, start
from one end..

..and then.. hey! no!
not the end of the cockerel's body..

...right.
the legs and that's it

now, you know the easy way to draw
a chicken, an egg and a cockerel

oh dear.. one of your drawings
fell over.. it doesn't really matter

er... you can easily
draw another cockerel
in one stroke if you like

bravo! it looks like a
real one! well, I've got
to go but please carry on.